Copyright © 2019 DC Comics.
DC SUPER HERO GIRLS and all related characters and elements
© & ™ DC Comics and Warner Bros. Entertainment Inc.
WB SHIELD: ™ & © WBEI. (s19)

Visit us on the Web!
rhcbooks.com
dcsuperherogirls.com
dckids.com

Library of Congress Cataloging-in-Publication Data
Names: David, Erica, author. | Mengert, Hollie, illustrator.
Title: Winner takes all! / by Erica David ; illustrated by Hollie Mengert.
Other titles: DC super hero girls.
Description: New York : Random House, [2019]
Identifiers: LCCN 2019020420 | ISBN 978-1-9848-9453-3 (paperback) |
ISBN 978-1-9848-9454-0 (lib. bdg.) | ISBN 978-1-9848-9455-7 (ebook)
Subjects: | BISAC: JUVENILE FICTION / Media Tie-In. | JUVENILE FICTION /
Humorous Stories.
Classification: LCC PZ7.D28197 Win 2019 | DDC [Fic]—dc23

Printed in the United States of America
10 9 8 7 6 5 4 3 2 1

Winner Takes All!

By Erica David
Illustrated by Hollie Mengert

Random House 🏠 New York

Chapter 1

Sometimes a Tiara Is Not Just a Tiara; It's a Challenge

Zee Zatara was the first to see Diana. As usual, Zee greeted Diana with a warm hug.

"Why didn't you tell me?" Zee asked dramatically. "I didn't even know that you were interested!"

Diana Prince's five closest friends, as well as a large group of their fellow students, were packed in at the end of the hall. Everyone was clustered around a bulletin board, reading the latest announcements. There seemed to be more excitement in the air than usual.

"Huh?" Diana said, puzzled. She had no idea what Zee was talking about, but she did know that her friend could be dramatic with a capital D. It was probably because Zee was the daughter and assistant of a famous stage magician. She was used to keeping an audience spellbound.

"The list just came out," Karen Beecher said softly. Karen was probably the quietest of

Diana's friends. She was the opposite of Zee when it came to drama.

"What list?" Diana asked.

"Actually, there are two lists. Such a waste of paper!" Jessica Cruz told her. Jessica was constantly on the lookout for ways to reduce, reuse, and recycle.

"Well, how else were they going to post the nominees?" asked Kara Danvers, but then quickly added, "I mean, not that I'm interested or anything." Kara was too much of a rebel to pay attention to bulletin board lists.

"I'd post by text alert," said Barbara Gordon, scrolling through her cell phone. "Babs," as she was known to her friends, was a whiz with gadgets and all things internet. "But nobody asked me."

"For Zeus's sake! Will someone please explain what is going on?" Diana asked.

Her five friends turned to look at her. They couldn't believe she didn't know. The school

was about to celebrate homecoming, a time of year when students new and old came to visit. Everyone pitched in to fix up the school for the occasion. It was a big deal! The celebration included pep rallies, a football game, and most importantly, a school dance.

"You do this every year?" Diana asked, after her friends explained the tradition. She was new to Metropolis and to the World of Man, as she called it. Diana was used to living among the Amazon warriors on a secret island called Themyscira. She excelled in hand-to-hand combat, but dancing the Macarena was a mystery to her.

"Of course!" said Zee. "It's tradition! We nominate outstanding students, then we vote for them to become the king and queen of homecoming."

Diana's eyes brightened when she heard the word "queen." Her mother, Hippolyta, was queen of the Amazons. She was a strong,

6

fierce ruler, and Diana wanted to impress her. "What does this homecoming queen do? Does she lead her people into battle?" she asked.

"Not unless battle requires a frilly dress," Kara said, blowing a wisp of her bangs out of her eyes.

"It's not that kind of queen. It's more of a ceremonial role," Babs explained. "Like a sprig of parsley next to a hot cheese quesadilla."

Diana moved closer to the cluster of students. She looked at the flyers on the board. There were two lists of nominees— one for homecoming king and the other for homecoming queen. Sure enough, her name was at the top of the list for queen.

"But we haven't told you the best part, Diana!" Zee chirped enthusiastically.

"You mean about the crown?" Babs said.

"Tiara! It's called a *tiara*," Zee said.

"Sounds like a fancy crown to me," Kara muttered.

7

"Well, it's different. This tiara has a special sapphire called the Star of Andromeda," Zee explained. "And it's famous! It even has its own legend!"

A hush fell over the students as Zee told the story of the tiara. Some people believed that the sapphire had magic powers. There was a rumor that it granted the wearer one wish every thousand years on the night of the full moon! It just so happened that the homecoming dance was on the thousand-year anniversary! "That means whoever wins queen gets a wish!" Zee finished.

"You don't *really* believe that, do you?" Kara asked skeptically.

Zee shrugged as if to say, "It's possible."

But for the other girls, it didn't matter if the story was true.

"I know what I'd wish for," said Jessica. "I'd wish to stop climate change."

"I'd wish to be the World's Greatest

Detective," said Babs.

"I'd wish people would listen when I ta—" Karen began.

"SQUEEEEEEEEEEEEEEEE!" a high-pitched voice interrupted.

Everyone turned to look in the direction of the sound. The squeal of delight had come from Carol Ferris, a cheerleader and devoted fan of the school's football team. Carol's name was also on the list for homecoming queen.

"Uh-oh, Carol is going to be fierce competition," Jessica whispered to Diana. "Everyone knows she has a huge crush on Hal Jordan, and he's up for homecoming king." Hal was Jessica's friend and quarterback of the football team. (He was also secretly a Green Lantern just like her.) "I bet she wants that crown so she can wish for Hal's undying love."

"Tiara," Zee said. "It's a tiara!"

Carol clasped her hands together and twirled joyfully on her tippy toes. It was as if she were floating on a cloud of happiness. But suddenly, she turned serious.

"Where's my crown?" Carol demanded. Her eyes were steely with determination.

Unfortunately for Carol, the tiara wasn't in the building. Zee explained that it was being kept at Larry Stinson Jewelers until the night of the dance. Stinson was the most famous jeweler in all of Metropolis.

"Slow down there, Carol. First, you have to be elected queen," Kara grumbled. "Or so I hear. I mean, not that I'm interested or anything."

"That's right," Zee said. She turned to Diana, who had her own ideas about being

queen. None of them involved tiaras. "I can't wait to get to work on your campaign, Diana. You'll let us help, right?"

"Of course." Diana nodded. "It will be a pleasure to have your help. Together we can ensure that the people elect a queen who will lead them on the path to justi—"

"SQUEEEEEEEEEEEEEEEEEEEEE!" a second, higher-pitched squeal emerged from the crowd. But this time it wasn't Carol. It was Oliver Queen, star of the school's drama club. He was thrilled to see his name on the list for homecoming king. Within seconds, he was campaigning. He stacked his textbooks on the floor and stood on top of them.

"My fellow students. It is my great honor to receive your nomination for homecoming king!" Oliver said earnestly.

"Oh boy. Here we go," Zee thought, rolling her eyes. She and Oliver were in drama club together—and *DRAMA* followed

Oliver wherever he went.

"There are many, many reasons why you should elect me your homecoming king. There're my good looks, my undeniable charisma, my winning nature, my flawless smile, my aquiline nose, my assertive and dry handshake, my so-called gift for gab, my perfect elocution," Oliver told the crowd, counting the reasons on his fingers.

"How long is this going to go on?" Diana whispered to Zee.

"How many fingers does he have?" Zee replied.

"I think he's running out," Babs said, looking at her own fingers and trying to keep track with Oliver.

"But he has toes!" Kara pointed out.

The rest of the students didn't seem to notice. This was their first glimpse of the campaign to come, and they were riveted.

". . . and my strong, stunning profile," Oliver continued. "But I want you to know that I'm more than just a pretty face. I'm a candidate of substance and unparalleled leadership ability, unlike some sleight-of-hand charlatans I know."

Zee's eyebrows drew together. She knew an insult when she heard one. It seemed as though their ongoing competition was still on.

When Oliver finished his speech and stepped down from his stack of books, he walked straight toward Diana, Zee, and the other girls. He was grinning from ear to ear.

"I didn't see your name on the list of nominees," Oliver said smugly to Zee.

"I prefer to work my magic behind the

scenes as Diana's campaign manager," Zee told him. "She's one hundred percent the best woman for the job!"

"And Zee Zatara is one hundred percent my charlatan of choice!" Diana said enthusiastically.

"Fair enough." Oliver chuckled. "Let the games begin!" He and Zee glared at one another for just a moment, and then Oliver

turned and walked off down the hall.

Diana watched him go, then turned to Zee. "It appears that this homecoming is serious business," she said.

"That's right," Zee replied. "And there isn't a moment to lose! We're not going to rest until that tiara is on your head!"

Chapter 2

Larry, Just So You Know, Sapphires Are a Cat's Best Friend

At the same time across town, there was one girl *not* in school. Selina Kyle hadn't been nominated for homecoming queen, and that was just fine with her. Being queen didn't interest her, but rare jewels did—and the Star of Andromeda was certainly a rare jewel.

Selina slipped stealthily into her secret hideout. It was the place where she kept all her treasures. Moments later, she found what she was looking for: a beautiful jewelry box. Slowly, Selina lifted the mirrored lid and pulled out the velvet-lined trays. Each tray held a priceless gemstone that she had "borrowed" from another home, a jewelry store, or a museum.

"Hello, my beauties," Selina said, greeting her jewels. She lifted a sparkling necklace dripping with diamonds from the box. This was Selina Kyle's deepest, darkest secret. When she wasn't skipping class or faking permission slips, she was the notorious cat burglar known as Catwoman.

Selina slipped the diamond necklace over her head and admired her reflection. "It's true what they say about diamonds," she whispered. "They really are a girl's best friend."

She returned the necklace to

its tray, only to pick up a glittering ruby the size of an egg. "Remember when I liberated you from the museum, my precious?" she told the gem. "That mean old Batman tried to keep us apart, but we make *purr*-fect companions."

The ruby seemed to wink at Selina in the sunlight. When it came to jewels, she just couldn't resist. "Soon, you'll have another little friend, my kitties. Very soon," she whispered to her gems.

Selina carefully returned the ruby and closed the jewelry box. It was time to set her plan in motion. It was time for her campaign for the tiara to begin.

Larry Stinson Jewelers was located in one of Metropolis's poshest neighborhoods. Selina could smell the fancy a mile away, and she wasn't disappointed when she stepped into the store's interior. Rays of sun filtered through

a beautiful stained-glass skylight in the ceiling, and sleek glass cases filled with expensive jewelry lined the walls. Customers spoke with sales associates in hushed tones, while classical music played softly in the background.

Gold glittered and diamonds twinkled. It was almost too easy for Selina to be distracted by the sheer number of precious gems, but she kept her focus. She walked straight to the rear of the store, where a lone display case sat in a pool of light. The tiara was perched on a pillow behind the glass. The blue sapphire in the center of the tiara was enormous! The Star of Andromeda reflected and refracted the light, bathing Selina's face in a cool blue glow.

"Can I help you?" asked a friendly salesperson.

"Yes. I couldn't help but notice this beautiful tiara," Selina said. "I was wondering if you could tell me about it."

"Certainly," said the salesperson, eager to please. "The Star of Andromeda is one of the largest star sapphires ever found. It weighs in at eight hundred carats!"

"Really?" said Selina, pretending to be impressed. The truth was she already knew all about the Star of Andromeda. She'd done her homework. She was only here to find out what she didn't know—where they kept the tiara at night.

"That's right," the salesperson said. "You know, this stone has an interesting history. Some say it once belonged to a famous warrior queen. Her king perished in battle. But she wished upon the sapphire, and it brought him back to life!"

"That's incredible!" Selina purred.

20

"Isn't it? They say the stone grants wishes."
He chuckled. "You wouldn't believe the things
we have to do to protect it."

"Like what?" Selina asked innocently.

"I really shouldn't be telling you this, but
we've got all sorts of security," the salesperson
explained. "There's the vault at the back of the
store, and then there are the motion detectors.
Every door and window is wired! The only
way in would be that skylight. But let's face it,
that's so high up, no one could get to it."

"Hmm," Selina murmured
thoughtfully. "That does
sound like a challenge."

"Even if someone did
get into the store, we
keep this beauty in the
vault at night."

"This tiara certainly is
well protected," Selina said slyly.

"Is there anything else I can help you with today, miss?"

"Just one more thing. How long will the Star of Andromeda be on display here?" Selina asked.

"Probably for another week or so. Then Larry Stinson is lending the tiara to Metropolis High for their homecoming dance," the salesperson said. "One lucky student will get to wear it for a few minutes. Say, you aren't one of the students in the running for the crown, are you?"

"Well, I really shouldn't tell you this," Selina whispered conspiratorially, "but let's just say I have no doubt that this crown will end up on my head."

"Good luck, then!" said the salesperson. He waved pleasantly to Selina as she left the store. He was completely unaware that he had just given valuable information to one of the most notorious cat burglars in all of Metropolis.

Chapter 3

These Boots Are
Made for Dancing . . .
and General Mayhem

As an Amazon princess, Diana loved to train. The Amazons were brave warriors who practiced their battle skills regularly. They scaled mountains and swam rivers. They did not, however, plié in dance studios.

"Are you sure this is the appropriate training for a queen?" Diana asked.

Zee, Kara, Karen, Babs, and Jessica had all gathered in the school's dance studio to help Diana prepare for her campaign. Not only would she have to make speeches and shake

23

hands, but she'd also have to learn the duties of a homecoming queen. One of those duties was dancing.

"Trust me, Diana. The homecoming king and queen always kick off the first dance," Zee explained. "You'll have to follow my lead."

"But I have excellent leadership abilities!" Diana said. "Did I ever tell you of the time when I entered the Tournament of Athena and Aphrodite, endured the Twenty-One Challenges, and earned the right to the title of 'Woman'?"

"YES!" Diana's friends chorused in unison. They had heard the story *many* times. As the youngest Amazon, Diana had been eager to prove her worthiness, especially to her mother, Queen Hippolyta. When the tribe of warriors had learned that the World of Man was in trouble, Hippolyta decided to send an Amazon champion to help. Diana had volunteered, but her mother thought she was too young.

Instead, the queen decided to hold a tournament with twenty-one of the most difficult challenges ever imagined. The winner of the tournament would become the champion. Diana entered the contest in disguise, hiding her identity. When Diana won, she revealed herself to her mother. Her heroic display had earned her the right to be known among her people by the title of "Woman." It also meant that she could travel to Metropolis and begin her journey as the champion of the World of Man . . . sort of. School came first.

"Then you know that I could never have won the tournament or made the perilous journey to your world without excellent leadership skills," Diana said.

"We get it, D. No one's questioning your leadership," Kara said. "It's just that all that Amazon stuff isn't quite the same."

"What she's saying is that a queen

needs to be light on her feet," said Zee.

"Ah, you speak of acrobatics. I think you will find that I am quite well versed in those," Diana told them.

Zee and Kara exchanged a look.

"Okay, let's begin with something simple," Zee said. She motioned to Babs, who tapped her phone. Suddenly, music piped out of the speakers in the dance studio. It was a slow, stately waltz. "Just feel the music. Let it move you."

Diana nodded eagerly. She listened to the rhythmic sweep of the music—one, two, three . . . one, two, three . . . one, two, three— and closed her eyes. Soon, she began to sway in time. She imagined that her feet moved with a warrior's precision and an acrobat's grace. She forgot all about her surroundings, and as she danced across the floor, she felt like she was floating.

Unfortunately for her friends, what Diana

imagined was very different from reality. Zee looked on, alarmed, as Diana's arms jerked and chopped through the air. Her legs kicked out at odd angles, seemingly of their own accord. As Diana neared the far corner of the studio, Karen had to tuck and roll to avoid being hit by one of Diana's loose limbs.

"EEEEP!" Karen cried.

But Diana didn't notice. With her eyes still closed, she veered suddenly to the left and accidentally collided with Jessica.

"Ow!" Jessica yelped, rubbing her shin.

Zee signaled to Babs to cut the music, but not before Diana had her grand finale. As the music built to a crescendo, so did her dance moves. She double-chopped with her left hand, kicked once with her right leg, and finished with a series of stomping steps that pounded the floor like a jackhammer.

"Whoa, there!" Zee said, once the music stopped.

Diana opened her eyes. What she saw left her puzzled. For some strange reason, all her friends were huddled behind Kara, using her as a shield.

"What do you think, Zee Zatara?" Diana asked cheerfully. "I have been told that I move with the grace of the nine muses."

"Which one of those muses has two left feet?" asked Babs. She thought about it for a moment as her mind raced, then got excited. Really excited. "WAIT! Who says muses even have feet? You don't need feet to muse. You just need a brain. A really BIG BRAIN! A MONDO brain, like the size of a Colossus! Like, so big it wouldn't even fit in a jar. But what *does* fit in a jar? PICKLES! And pickles DON'T DANCE!"

Zee and Diana blinked, both were confused.

"You've got to think like a person, not a pickle," Babs said as though the answer had been staring them in the face the whole time.

Zee patted Babs on the shoulder, then turned to Diana.

"Your style of dance is very, um . . . *interesting,*" she said politely. "But it seems like maybe you're used to dancing alone. The homecoming queen usually dances with the homecoming king."

Zee suggested that Diana try practicing with a dance partner. But when she asked for a volunteer, everyone quickly huddled behind Kara again.

"Kara, looks like you're up," Zee told her.

While the other girls were hesitant to partner with Diana, Kara wasn't worried. Her superstrength meant that she could survive

Diana's moves without getting hurt . . . much. She stepped forward and, doing her best homecoming king impression, swept a deep bow in front of Diana.

"May I have this dance?" Kara asked jokingly.

"Excellent!" Zee said. "Now, remember, Diana, the boy usually leads."

"Why does the boy lead?" asked Diana. "I have excellent leadership abilities! Did I ever tell you of the time when I entered the Tournament of—"

"YES!" everyone answered.

"It's tradition that the boy leads," Zee said.

"But it doesn't always mean he's the best leader," Kara added. She offered Diana her hand and tugged her into a ballroom dancing stance. "Babs, cue the music!"

Another waltz began to play. Kara and Diana set out across the dance floor. At first, the two girls looked evenly matched. If every

once in a while Diana accidentally stepped on her friend's foot, Kara didn't seem to notice. But then a strange thing happened. When Kara wanted to go one way, Diana wanted to go the other.

"This way!" Kara said.

"No, this way!" Diana replied.

Kara gripped her friend's hand and spun her across the floor. Unfortunately, she didn't know her own strength. Diana twirled so quickly that she accidentally bounced off the wall!

"Yikes!" said Karen.

But Diana didn't mind. Enthusiastically, she took Kara's hand again. It was her turn to send Kara flying—literally! She tossed Kara so hard that she flew across the room, floating above the ground!

"Careful, Diana!" Zee called. But it made no difference. The two girls were locked in a spirited tango.

"Let me dip you!" Kara said.

"No, let *me* dip *you*!" Diana insisted.

Zee had seen enough. For everyone's safety, she stepped between the two girls. It was clear to Zee that Diana needed more than a strong partner if she was going to learn to dance elegantly. Diana needed a bit of magic.

"Ecnad, ecnad!" Zee said, casting a spell on Diana's shoes. In no time, Diana glided gracefully across the floor. Kara, Babs, Jessica, and Karen were pleasantly surprised by what they saw. This Diana turned perfect pirouettes and was no longer in danger of accidentally clobbering her friends!

Karen was the first to realize this. She

partnered with Diana and led her in a graceful waltz. Soon, Diana was dancing with each of her friends, flowing elegantly from one girl to the next. But suddenly, her feet began to move faster and faster. She swirled and twirled so quickly that none of her friends could keep up.

"Slow down, Diana!" Jessica huffed, dancing as fast as she could.

"I am trying!" Diana said. But her enchanted boots had other ideas.

"Uh-oh," said Zee. She was still getting used to her magical powers, and her spells sometimes went haywire. Now Diana's feet were moving so quickly that they had almost become a blur! The rest of her body struggled to keep up.

"Stop these shoes, Zee Zatara!" Diana shouted.

Zee tried to reverse the spell, but every time she got close, Diana's rapidly churning feet carried her away. Her shoes danced her out of the studio and into the hall.

"Come back, Diana!" Zee called, running after her. The other girls followed.

In the hallway, students scattered when they saw Diana approach. Her arms and legs flailed wildly. She accidentally dented lockers and sent homework flying. Worst of all, she was on a collision course with Hal Jordan, who was standing by his locker.

Hal heard the commotion and saw Diana careening down the hall. But what looked like trouble to everyone else looked like fun to Hal. As Diana grew near, Hal spun left, dodged right, and ducked nimbly. His fancy footwork from the football field came in handy. When he spun and darted around Diana, it almost looked like the two of them were dancing.

"Go figure," Jessica said to Zee as they caught up. "Hal Jordan is the perfect partner."

Zee took advantage of everyone staring at the two dancers and beamed a spell in Diana's direction. "Teef tlah!"

The magic worked! All at once, the boots stopped moving. Diana was caught off guard by the sudden stop. She lost her balance and keeled over into Hal's arms.

Hal quickly returned Diana to her feet. "Next time, how about letting me lead?" he joked.

"Thank you, but that is not necessary," Diana answered. "I have excellent leadership abilities."

"Step away from him!" Carol Ferris shouted from across the hall. She had witnessed the whole incident, and she wasn't happy. The cheerleader walked toward Diana with a determined gait. "You will not have him! I

WILL BE QUEEN. AND HAL JORDAN WILL BE MY KING!"

"I do not need Hal Jordan. He is useless in battle," Diana replied.

"Hey!" Hal said indignantly.

"He will be mine!" said Carol. It made no difference that Hal was slowly backing away from her.

Zee stepped in and took Diana's arm. She quickly led Diana down the hall, leaving Hal to deal with Carol. There were more important things to worry about. After all, homecoming was at stake!

Chapter 4

Heavy Lies the Crown
(So Don't Try to Lift It)

Night fell over Metropolis. While most of its citizens were fast on their way to sleep, Selina Kyle tiptoed across the roof of Larry Stinson Jewelers, dressed in a sleek black suit and mask. Selina Kyle was now Catwoman.

She prowled through the shadows until she stood over the store's elaborate stained-glass skylight. She thought it would be a pity to ruin such a beautiful work of art, but that didn't stop her from doing what she did next. She bared her sharp metal claws.

Within moments she'd carved a hole in the glass just wide enough for her to fit through. Catwoman peered down through the opening into the store below. She dropped a rope through the hole and slithered down into the store.

Like most cats, Catwoman landed on her feet with barely a sound. She stood in front of the empty glass case where she'd first seen the Star of Andromeda. Beams of red light crisscrossed the air all around her. They were motion detectors.

"Well, if it isn't the cat's cradle," Catwoman said smugly. She knew that it would take more than a fancy light show to stop her. In just a

few seconds, she had slipped easily through the laser beams to the vault where the jewels were kept at night.

Catwoman had to admit that the vault was impressive. It had a huge round door at least eight feet thick made of solid steel. A less-experienced thief might have been nervous, but she wasn't worried—cracking safes was her specialty. Slowly, she spun the metal wheel on the outside of the door and listened to the tumblers in the lock. It was as if they told her what to do. In no time, the lock clicked, and the heavy steel door swung open.

"Child's play," Catwoman said with a satisfied smirk. "Or should I say *cat's* play?"

Her smirk faded, however, when she stepped into the vault. There, with her hands poised to lift the tiara from its case, was the super-villain known as Star Sapphire! Star had used her powers as a Violet Lantern to enter the vault without leaving a trace.

"Well, well, well. Two sapphires instead of one," Catwoman drawled. In fact, she knew the second sapphire quite well. "I wasn't expecting you here, Carol."

Carol Ferris huffed, annoyed. "I told you not to call me that, Selina!" she said. "It's Star."

"Well, Star, what do you want with *my* tiara?" Catwoman asked.

"*Your* tiara? You don't deserve this tiara!" Star snapped, reaching for it.

"No, don't—" Catwoman warned her. But it was too late. As soon as Star Sapphire lifted the tiara from its case, a loud siren wailed. She had tripped the alarm.

Catwoman knew that there wasn't a moment to spare. The police would be on their way. She rushed over to Star Sapphire and grabbed the tiara. But Star wasn't going to give up so easily. She held tight to the tiara. The two villains were quickly caught in a tug-of-war!

"Give me that!" Star Sapphire hissed.

"Let go, you purple pest!" Catwoman snarled as the two of them tumbled out of the open vault. "This is no time to argue!"

Catwoman and Star Sapphire got so caught up in their fight over the tiara that they didn't hear the sound of justice approaching.

"Halt and unhand that crown!"

Catwoman and Star Sapphire turned.

"Wonder Woman!" they both gasped.

Wonder Woman stood with her hands on her hips, her long dark hair flowing over her shoulders. Behind her, the rest of the super hero girls stood ready to rumble.

The villains forgot their fight over the tiara for the moment. Star Sapphire cut loose with a heart-shaped energy blast from her power ring. The super hero girls dodged it. Catwoman used the momentary distraction to make a run for it. She sped through the store, ignoring the motion detectors. When she reached the front door, she smashed through it with a flying kick.

Star Sapphire wasn't about to be left behind. With her Violet Lantern powers, she created a heart-shaped cloud, hopped on board, and flew through the store. She rose through the hole in the skylight and escaped into the night.

"Not so fast, sweetheart," said Supergirl, flying after her. Green Lantern and Bumblebee followed, while Batgirl, Zatanna, and Wonder Woman chased Catwoman.

Catwoman was quick and nimble. She led the heroes back through the store and out into the dark streets of Metropolis. The only light came from the moon overhead. It cast shadows that made the perfect cover for a cat burglar on the run.

"I do love a stroll in the moonlight," Catwoman said. "But I *purr*-fer to take it alone." With that, she knocked over a row of trash cans and sent them rolling toward her pursuers. Wonder Woman, Batgirl, and Zatanna dodged them easily, but not before

Catwoman ducked into an alley.

"Oh great. We're in for a night of cat puns—and me without my thesaurus," Zatanna said.

"It's a *cat*-tastrophe!" Batgirl joked.

Wonder Woman hurried into the alley after Catwoman and saw her climbing up a fire escape on the side of an old warehouse. She uncoiled her Lasso of Truth, twirled it over her head, and hurled it at the thief. The lasso narrowly missed, but Wonder Woman looped it around the fire escape and swung herself up after the villain.

"Still there?" Catwoman asked, glancing over her shoulder. "Why, you're positively *purr*-sistent, aren't you?"

"Great Zeus! This is no time for wordplay!" Wonder Woman said.

"Did you say 'play'? Could I interest you in a game of cat and mouse?" asked Catwoman.

"How about cat and *bat*?" said Batgirl, climbing up behind them. The three girls

reached the rooftop, where Zatanna was already waiting.

"What can I say? The perks of teleportation," she said. "Looks like you're surrounded, Whiskers."

"Don't you know it's not wise to corner a cat?" said Catwoman.

Suddenly, Star Sapphire flew overhead on her heart-shaped cloud. Supergirl and Bumblebee zoomed after her, with Green Lantern following in a hang-glider construct powered by her power ring.

Star Sapphire swooped down toward Catwoman. Just when it looked as if she was going to rescue Catwoman, she plucked the tiara from her head!

"Are you *kitten* me?!" Catwoman snarled.

Supergirl tore off after Star Sapphire. With a burst of superspeed, she caught up with her and punched a hole through the heart-shaped

cloud. The force of the blow knocked the tiara out of Star Sapphire's hands.

"Sorry to break your heart," Supergirl said. "Actually? Not sorry."

"Noooooooooooooooo!" Star Sapphire cried.

The world's most expensive sapphire tumbled through the air.

"I got it, I got it, I got it," said Bumblebee. The wings in her suit beat double-time as she zipped after the tiara. All eyes were on her.

Catwoman saw that this was a good time to make her escape. With everyone distracted, she tiptoed off into the night.

Knowing that she was outnumbered, Star Sapphire shot straight up and disappeared into the night sky, becoming a small purple pinpoint of light in the distance.

"Careful, Bumblebee!" Wonder Woman called. The tiara was falling fast and headed straight for the ground. Bumblebee dove. Everyone held their breath. It seemed like

she'd never reach it in time. But at the last possible second, she snagged the tiara before it splintered into a thousand pieces.

The super hero girls breathed huge sighs of relief. It wasn't until everyone was safely back on the ground that they noticed the villains were gone.

"It's just as well," Batgirl said, snickering. "If they'd stuck around, they would have been in *tiara*-ble trouble."

The others groaned. They all agreed that it was definitely time to call it a night, as soon as the tiara was returned to its rightful owner.

Chapter 5

The Queen Who Would Be King . . . (It'll Make More Sense When You Read the Chapter)

Though the midnight heist had kept the super hero girls up late, they managed to arrive on time for school the next day. As Babs, Jessica, and Zee walked in through the building's tall double doors, they were unprepared for what would greet them.

Oliver Queen's face beamed down at them from every available surface. His colorful campaign posters were plastered all over the walls and bulletin boards. The posters read VOTE QUEEN FOR KING! and featured Oliver smiling from ear to ear.

"Somebody wake me from this nightmare!" Zee said, annoyed. "It's like he's taken over the school!"

"'Queen for king!'" Babs said with a snort of dorky laughter. She couldn't help but appreciate the catchy slogan.

Zee was not amused. "When will Diana's posters be ready, Jess?" she asked.

"In a couple of days," Jessica answered. "The printer has the recycled paper in stock, but they're still waiting on the eco-friendly ink."

Zee scowled at the posters blanketing the walls. She was so focused on them that she almost didn't notice the T-shirts. Almost.

"What on earth?!" she exclaimed.

A large group of students walked by all wearing "Queen for king" T-shirts. Still more had Oliver Queen buttons pinned to their backpacks and jackets. Then there were the key chains, phone charms, and stickers. One lucky student even carried a program from the school play autographed by Oliver himself!

"Great guacamole!" Babs said. "Oliver is really good at putting his face on stuff."

"Luckily for us, it takes more than putting your face on stuff to win a campaign," said Zee.

"Does it?" asked Babs. "I mean, that is *a lot* of stuff."

Diana carried her lunch tray over to where Zee, Babs, and Jessica were sitting with Kara and Karen. She wanted to meet with her friends during lunch to go over the next steps for her campaign. At least, that was the plan, until Karen used a napkin to wipe a bit of broccoli from her face.

"Stop right there!" Zee shouted.

Karen froze with the napkin still held to her mouth. She had no idea what was going on.

"I don't believe it!" Zee gasped incredulously. "His face is even on the napkins!"

Sure enough, Oliver Queen's image stared

back at them from all the paper products in the school cafeteria.

"How in the name of spicy salsa did he do that?" asked Babs.

"Why did he do that?" asked Kara. "Who puts face on a napkin?"

Oddly enough, Diana seemed to like the napkin. "It is both helpful and absorbent."

"I don't think absorbent is what people look for in a homecoming king," Karen said softly.

"Right you are, young Karen!" said Oliver's voice.

"Oh jeez, the napkin's talking!" Karen squealed. She quickly balled it up in her fist.

"It's not the napkin, it's me!" Oliver said. Karen turned to see him standing right behind her. "And you're right, absorption isn't everything. That's why I've got a forty-seven-point plan for success!"

Oliver set his tray down and climbed up onto the table next to Karen. He cleared his

throat and called for attention using the skills he'd perfected in the school play.

"Friends, Metropolitans, countrymen, lend me your ears," Oliver began. "We are gathered here today to think about the choice we must all make when it comes to electing a homecoming king. I want to assure you that not only will I dance divinely and look dashing in my crown, but I will also work tirelessly to

improve the school with my forty-seven-point plan for school beautification. Point number one: I promise you two-ply toilet paper in the restrooms. . . ."

"He can't possibly list all forty-seven points, can he?" Jessica whispered to Babs.

"Shhhhhh!" Babs said. "I want to hear about this toilet paper thing."

Zee cut Babs an angry look.

"*What?* One-ply is scratchy," Babs said sheepishly.

Oliver's speech went on and on. Zee did her best to mask her frustration, but she wasn't succeeding. Her face went from red to purple with rage. Diana's cheeks remained a healthy pink, however. She found Oliver's speech inspiring—all twenty-plus minutes of it.

"And so, my fellow students, in conclusion, I say this before you cast your ballots next week: ask not what your homecoming king can do for you, ask what you can do for your

homecoming king!" Oliver said grandly.

The cafeteria broke out into wild applause. Students waved their napkins above their heads and chanted, "Queen for king! Queen for king! Queen for king!"

"Quickly, Diana," Zee said over the cheering. "This is the perfect time to make a speech. Don't let Oliver steal the show."

Diana nodded. She liked the idea of addressing her fellow students and was eager to share her thoughts. She climbed up onto the lunch table and gazed out over the cafeteria.

"My fellow students. Citizens of Metropolis," Diana said in a strong, commanding voice. "By Hera's shining justice, it is my great honor to be nominated as your homecoming leader. A leader should be forged from the heart of battle and willing to conquer all obstacles. She should smite all enemies, like the mighty Hercules and the huntress Diana, for whom I am named. Guided by Athena's wisdom, I have many ideas for improvements to this, our fortress of learning. It is my hope that we can summon the spirit of mutual school pride and forge a coalition of warrior-scholars dedicated to the renovation of our facilities—"

"Less Greek, more geek," Babs whispered, tugging at Diana's skirt. "Actually—and I never thought I'd say this—less geek, too."

Zee covered her face with her hands. This

was not going as she had pictured. And it kept going. And going. Diana kept talking.

"I pledge to lead with the strength of the hammer and the resilience of the anvil—"

"What's an anvil?" Karen asked Jessica. Jessica shrugged.

"Life often presents us with challenges," Diana continued. "Twenty-one challenges, in fact—"

"WE KNOW!" her friends said. Kara took advantage of the interruption to give Diana the wrap-it-up hand signal.

"In conclusion, I am also highly absorbent. Thank you," she said, stepping down with an enthusiastic smile. Diana was proud of herself. Her chance to address the public was everything she'd imagined.

The entire lunchroom sat in stunned silence. They didn't know what to make of Diana's speech. Babs, Kara, Jessica, Karen, and Zee exchanged looks across the lunch table. They knew that something had to be done.

Suddenly, Babs sprang to her feet. "YEEEEAAAAAAAAHHHHH! Let's hear it for Diana! She's really got a way with words—which are the ultimate form of communication. Words are like sound and sense all wrapped up in one. They're like the SONIC BURRITOS of our existence, and Diana SPEAKS BURRITO!" Babs pumped her fist in the air in time to a beat only she could hear. "I mean, who's not up for a night of righteous smiting? Am I right?"

"Totally!" said Zee, catching on. "And did you hear Diana's school improvement plan? It's the smeltiest! Like, smelt city!"

"So smelty!" Karen chimed in.

The students in the cafeteria began to murmur. Moments later, the murmur became a buzz. Everyone was trying out Diana's way with words.

"I'm gonna let slip the dogs of war on that math test."

60

"If my locker keeps sticking, I'm gonna smite it with a thunderbolt."

"And then Coach went full Gorgon on the basketball team."

Jessica rose to her feet. "You've heard of a mic drop? Well, Diana's going to totally drop the anvil of Hephaestus!" she said.

"Anvil drop! Anvil drop! Anvil drop!" Kara said, chanting. The other girls joined in, pounding the table. Soon, the entire cafeteria caught the rhythm. They chanted and cheered for Diana, which made even Oliver Queen stand up and take notice.

Chapter 6

Follow the Leader—
But If the Leader You Are
Following Is Catwoman,
You're Probably a Villain

Selina Kyle wasn't the type to sit around and lick her wounds. After her run-in with the super hero girls at Larry Stinson Jewelers, she'd learned a thing or two. There were six of them and only one of her. The odds were not in her favor. The only way to even the score was to call on a few friends of her own. Selina used the term "friends" lightly, however. She knew that the old saying was true: there is no honor among thieves.

Fortunately, her fellow thieves were also her classmates. During science lab, Selina passed a note to Leslie Willis, Doris Zeul, Harleen Quinzel, and Pam Isley, asking them to meet her after school. The note was written in code, but the message was clear—this would be a meeting of super-villains. Capes and tights were required.

Catwoman was the first to arrive at the abandoned factory. When Leslie walked in as Livewire, the air crackled with electricity. She was followed by Doris's alter ego, Giganta, who was always large and in charge. Then Harleen arrived as Harley Quinn, the wisecracking life of the party. She overshadowed Pam Isley, whose green-thumbed secret identity, Poison Ivy, liked plants more than she did people.

With everyone assembled, Catwoman got down to business. "My fellow villains," she said, "I have a proposal."

"Lay it on us, Kit Cat," said Harley Quinn.

Catwoman told the girls about the Star of Andromeda. Since her attempt to steal the legendary sapphire, it had been moved to a new location. No one knew where it was, but Catwoman had a plan to find out.

"What's in it for us?" Giganta asked. "I don't need no stinkin' tiara."

"Even one that grants wishes?" Catwoman purred.

"Aw, you'd have to be nutso to believe that!" said Harley Quinn.

"Let's hear her out," said Livewire, sparks glinting in her eyes. "I get a charge out of a good fairy tale."

"They say it grants the wearer one wish under the full moon every one thousand years," said Catwoman.

"One wish? There's five of us," Poison Ivy pointed out.

"I can count. That's why I'm suggesting we each take a turn wearing the crown," Catwoman drawled.

Giganta folded her meaty arms across her chest. She was skeptical. Catwoman wasn't known for sharing.

"Just think, Giganta. How'd you like to be even bigger and stronger than you are now?" Catwoman asked. "Even more . . . gigantic."

Giganta's mouth stretched into a greedy smile.

"Or you, Harley. Couldn't you use a wish to meet the Joker in person?" asked Catwoman.

Harley Quinn's eyes brightened at the thought.

"And what about you, Poison Ivy?" Catwoman said softly. "Imagine a world where plants rule and humans drool. One wish and it's all yours."

Poison Ivy perked up like a plant that had just been watered.

"Is that a spark of interest I see, Livewire?" Catwoman whispered.

"I don't know," Livewire said. "Who says this wish thing is even real?"

"Even if you don't believe in wish-granting tiaras, there's always the chance to make a bunch of your classmates sad when there's no fancy crown for their little homecoming party," Catwoman said. "And if the super hero girls happen to get in the way, well, you'll get all the satisfaction of clobbering them."

"Heh heh, clobbering," Giganta snickered.

This was a point that all the villains could agree on—clobbering the super hero girls was more than worth it. This wasn't the first time they would join forces against the good guys, and it wouldn't be the last. Only, this time, it seemed like they were one villain shy of a decent heist.

"Hey, where's Star?" Livewire asked.

"It seems that Star Sapphire's obsession with Hal Jordan has clouded her judgment," Catwoman said, rolling her eyes. "She wants the tiara all for herself. I'm afraid she's just not willing to share."

"Hal Jordan? What a dud," said Giganta.

"I agree. He's completely useless in battle. But to each her own," Catwoman replied with a shrug.

With the matter settled, she laid out her plan to locate the tiara. To find it, they'd have to pay a visit to the man himself: Larry Stinson.

Diana Prince also had a proposal to share. But unlike Catwoman, she met with her friends out in the open, on the practice field at school. Zee, Karen, Jessica, Kara, and Babs set their backpacks on the bleachers and walked over to Diana at midfield. She was standing next to a row of football tackling dummies.

"Thank you all for coming," Diana said.

"Sure. But who invited them?" Babs joked, pointing to the dummies.

"They are my special guests, Barbara Gordon. You will see," Diana said. "But first, I must share something with you. In the cafeteria, I realized I will need more training to be your homecoming queen."

"If this is about your speech . . . ," said Zee.

"No, it is not about the speech. As Barbara said, I have a way with words. This is about leadership and excellence," Diana explained.

"I must be worthy if I hope to win the crown."

"Something tells me you were born worthy," Kara said with a smirk.

"It is true that I am of noble birth," Diana replied. "But leadership must be proven. And what better way to prove my leadership than a rigorous exercise in teamwork!"

It wasn't exactly clear what Diana meant until she pointed to the tackling dummies on the field. They were part of an obstacle course she had set up. There were also hurdles, a tire run, a hand ladder, and even a few hoops to jump through. In the name of teamwork, Diana had designed a practice drill for the girls.

"You want us to tackle things?" Jessica asked.

"I want us to rely on one another and my excellent leadership skills to conquer all that stands in the path of justice," Diana answered. "It's the best training for a queen that I can think of."

"It's not really that kind of quee—" Babs reminded her.

Diana silenced her with a hand. "If we can work together at school on the field, then, by great Hera, we can work together after school, fighting crime on the streets of Metropolis!"

Diana lined everyone up at the start of the obstacle course. They would all have to communicate with each other if they hoped to make it through. Diana blew the whistle that hung around her neck to signal the start. Zee, Babs, Jessica, Kara, and Karen took off for the first obstacle.

"Wait! We need to strategize!" Diana called. But her friends didn't hear her.

The first obstacle was a tire run. Jessica was the first to reach it. She lifted her knees high as she hopped through the tires. Kara was impatient, though. She caught up to Jessica with her superspeed and accidentally knocked her out of the way!

Babs was the next to run through the tires. As she reached the end, her phone rang, and she stopped to answer it. She was completely unaware that Karen and Zee were right behind her. When she stopped, they crashed into her.

"We must communicate!" Diana shouted to her team from the sidelines.

The next challenge was the hurdles. Kara used her powers to fly over them, while Zee chose to magic them out of her way. But her spell backfired. The hurdles danced toward her and the other girls instead of away from them!

"Help!" Karen cried as three hurdles chased her.

Jessica powered up her Green Lantern ring and created a rope construct. She lassoed the three hurdles in an attempt to keep them from trampling Karen. But the hurdles bucked and reared like wild horses, dragging Jessica around the field through the grass and mud.

"By Hera's crown!" Diana exclaimed.

Zee hurried after Jessica and the hurdles, casting spells left and right. One spell ricocheted and hit Kara, freezing her so that she couldn't move! Eventually, Zee stopped the hurdles, but unfreezing Kara was more complicated.

Only Karen had made it far enough to reach the football dummies—the last obstacle in the

course. She squared her shoulders and ran straight toward them, hoping to drive them back. Unfortunately, her toe caught on a bit of loose turf. She stumbled and ended up sprawled out on the field. Meanwhile, Babs, having finished her phone call, ran toward the last obstacle. She didn't see Karen, though, and tripped right over her. That set off a chain reaction of bumbling and stumbling that left the girls piled up in a tangle of arms and legs.

From the bottom of the pile, Karen peeked out and saw Diana's feet approach.

"This was not what I had in mind," Diana said. She helped her friends up. Everyone dusted themselves off.

Kara, newly unfrozen, was first to speak. "So much for teamwork."

Diana was puzzled. She and her friends worked together all the time. Just the other day, they had foiled Catwoman's attempted robbery. She'd thought her obstacle course

73

would only improve their cooperation. "Maybe I should lead you in the Amazon way," she told her friends. "Our training produces legendary warriors."

"What kind of training is that?" Jessica asked uncertainly.

"First, we quarry one thousand pounds of stone from the mines of Hephaestus. Next, we muck out the stables of Chiron. Then we clean up after Cerberus."

"We don't have mines," said Babs.

"Or stables," said Kara.

"Or a Cerberus," said Karen. "What's a Cerberus?"

"Hmm, this presents a challenge," Diana said. But true to her nature, she found the challenge exciting. She looked out over the field, deep in thought. That was when she saw the old greenhouse behind the school gym and was struck by a brilliant idea. "We will fix up the greenhouse!" she said. "I will lead you, and we will work together to improve the school. It is the perfect training!"

"I like it," said Zee. "After all, school improvements are your campaign promise."

"I like it, too," said Karen. "There're no hurdles. Or tackling. Or Cerberuses-es."

Everyone followed Diana across the field to the greenhouse. The building was made entirely of glass, which let the sunlight shine through. The glass was dirty, though, and some panes were missing, so Diana assigned everyone a repair task. Kara and Jessica looked for replacement glass, Babs and Zee swept and cleaned, and Karen and Diana were in charge of planting. It would take some time, but if they worked hard, the greenhouse would be fixed in time for homecoming.

As Kara and Jessica worked to replace the missing glass, Kara heard a strange sound coming from far away. Her superhearing told her that it was the sound of a citizen in distress!

"Hey, it's go time!" Kara told her friends. "Someone's in danger!"

Diana, Zee, Kara, Babs, Jessica, and Karen enthusiastically sprang into action. Justice was calling, and far be it from the super hero girls to ignore the call.

Chapter 7

Brute Force. Truth Serums. Tickle Torture. The Villains Have Most Definitely Arrived.

Famous jeweler Larry Stinson knew the sound of a citizen in distress—most likely because he *was* a citizen in distress. In his penthouse in one of Metropolis's nicest neighborhoods, he found himself surrounded by a crew of crooks. Catwoman, Giganta, Livewire, Poison Ivy, and Harley Quinn had barged in and tied him up.

"What do you want?" he asked angrily. "I don't keep any jewels here!"

"We want ya to talk!" Harley Quinn said.

"And we have ways of making you," Livewire threatened. She nodded to Giganta, who grinned and cracked her knuckles.

"Tell us where you're keeping the Star of Andromeda and we'll be out of your hair," Catwoman said.

Larry shook his head. He wasn't about to give up such valuable information about his valuables.

"What's the matter, Larry? Cat got your tongue?" Catwoman asked. When Larry didn't answer, she gave a dramatic sigh. "Looks like we'll have to resort to other measures."

Beside her, Giganta pounded her big fist into her palm menacingly. As the strongest of the villains, she was prepared to exercise

her muscle if necessary. But before she could make a move, Poison Ivy stepped forward. A winding vine trailed after her. It uncurled to reveal a beautiful pale blue blossom.

"Not everything needs to be about brute force, Giganta. Why not try a little flower power?" Poison Ivy suggested. "One whiff of this blossom and Larry here will have to tell us the truth."

"A truth-serum plant? I didn't come all this way to let the front lawn fight my battles. I think it's time for a bit of shock treatment," Livewire said, shooting sparks from the tips of her fingers.

"Hold your horsies!" said Harley Quinn. "I got just the thing." She pulled a feather from her pocket and waved it threateningly.

"I don't get it," said Giganta. "How's the feather gonna clobber him?"

"We're not going to clobber him," said Catwoman, catching on to Harley's idea. "We're going to use *tickle* torture. Get him, Harl!"

Harley Quinn gave a gleeful shriek of delight. She closed in on Larry, who squirmed desperately in his chair. As soon as the tip of the feather touched his feet, he squealed with terrified laughter.

It was this sound that traveled across the city. With her super-hearing, Kara had heard it, and she led the super hero girls to Larry's penthouse. They arrived in the nick of time. Larry was extremely ticklish and was giggling so hard that he was about to

reveal the tiara's new location, when Wonder Woman, Supergirl, Batgirl, Green Lantern, Zatanna, and Bumblebee crashed through the large windows in his living room.

"If it ain't the super hero *squirrels!*" Harley Quinn cackled.

"No squirrels here. Just bats," said Batgirl, hurling a Batarang at Harley Quinn. It whisked through the air, tore the feather from Harley's hand, and pinned it to the wall behind her.

"Aw, rats, Bats! Yer ruinin' my fun," Harley griped. "*Un*lucky for you, I don't hold a grudge, I hold a mallet!" The villain pulled out a huge mallet and took a swing at Batgirl, who ducked and evaded the blow.

The other girls leaped into action. Supergirl flew straight toward Larry, hoping to untie him. But a large muscled arm shot out to block her path. Giganta stepped into view—all seven feet of her.

Supergirl wasn't intimidated. She flexed her muscles and readied herself for a fight.

Meanwhile, Wonder Woman tried to reason with the villains. "This juvenile behavior is foolish," she said. "Let this man go and turn yourselves in!"

"Not a chance, pussycat," said Catwoman, taking a swipe at Wonder Woman with her claws. Wonder Woman blocked the claws with her gauntlets and took a few swings of her own. Catwoman cartwheeled out of the way, dodging Wonder Woman's punches.

Behind them, Poison Ivy sent a web of vines slithering after Green Lantern. The hero channeled her power through her ring to create a glowing green trellis. The vines tangled themselves in the garden fence, deflecting the attack. Seconds later, Zatanna joined her friend and cast a spell that froze the vines solid. She pulled a penny from behind Green Lantern's ear, flicked it at the plants, and watched as the small coin shattered the frozen vines to pieces.

In the middle of it all, Larry Stinson did his best to avoid being accidentally crushed. He tried to inch his chair away from the fighting, especially when Giganta went flying past him, courtesy of Supergirl. The supersized villain hit the wall with a thud, leaving a body-shaped hole in the plaster. Larry squeezed his eyes shut, hoping it would all be over soon.

"Don't worry, sir," Bumblebee said. She

shrank down to the size of an insect, r o c k e t e d through the commotion, and landed next to him. In a flash, she grew to full size again and began to untie Larry's hands. Unfortunately, Livewire wasn't about to let that happen. She launched a bolt of electricity at Bumblebee, forcing her to dive for cover. Larry's hair stood on end as the energy flowed past him.

At the opposite side of the room, Wonder Woman spun and kicked, driving Catwoman toward the large windows. The wily thief flipped backward onto the window ledge and smirked. "You may be in the catbird seat for now, *Blunder* Woman. But it's true what they say about cats—we do have nine lives." With that, she jumped off the ledge and disappeared.

When the other villains saw Catwoman leave, they knew it was time to retreat. One by one they leaped out the windows, leaving just as quickly as they'd arrived.

"So much for the goon squad," Supergirl said.

With the villains gone, the super hero girls freed Larry Stinson and helped him up. He

explained that Catwoman and her crew had been after the location of the tiara. Fortunately, he hadn't told the villains anything useful, but that didn't mean the danger was over.

"We will have to be on our best guard at the homecoming dance," Wonder Woman said. The night of the dance was when the tiara was scheduled to make its next appearance. And all of Metropolis would be watching.

Chapter 8

Treat Yourself to a Selfie with Oliver Queen— He Will Make You Look Good!

With just a few days until the homecoming dance, the whole school was abuzz with excitement and anticipation. There were so many activities taking place that it was hard to keep track of them all. Fortunately, one plucky student took it upon herself to keep everyone up to date.

"Lois Lane here, bringing you the scoop, the skinny, the scuttlebutt live via social media for the *Daily Planetoid.*" Lois was the school's ace investigative reporter. She knew everything about everything, and if there was anything she didn't know, she made it her business to find out.

Today Lois was waiting for a closed-door meeting of the school's dance committee to let out. "All the school's caught it: dance fever! And it'll take more than the usual sock-hop shenanigans to cure what ails 'em," said Lois. "That's right, folks! The kids are crazy for choreography, and in the midst of all the homecoming hoopla, they want to know: What will the theme for the dance be?"

The door to the meeting room swung open and several students trickled out. Lois rushed forward, angling with her cell phone for the perfect shot. "Excuse me, excuse me!" she said, stopping the first student to exit the room. "Say, kid, don't leave this reporter in the dark. What's the homecoming theme?"

The student told Lois that the committee

hadn't reached a decision yet. She wanted an outer space theme featuring papier-mâché planets, but the other members were split. Lois looked at those other members as they left the room. Garth Bernstein and Barbi Minerva walked out at the same time, but they were far from together.

Barbi was known for being rich and popular, while Garth was known for being, well . . . neither of those things. But he did work at a pet store and liked fish very much.

"Miss Minerva, spare a second for the press! What's the theme for homecoming?" asked Lois.

"It's all about luxury, Lois, darling," Barbi drawled. "My idea is Puttin' On the Ritz. Crystal, chandeliers, gold leaf, the works."

"Sounds expensive," said Lois. "And you, Garth?"

"I have this great idea for an underwater theme. You know, with an aquarium and

90

sea ladies and clams and kelp streamers—"

"*Boring!*" said Barbi Minerva. "Who wants to spend the night tangled in seaweed?"

"There you have it, folks. The debate rages on," Lois said. She was just about to end her broadcast when she spotted Diana, Zee, and Jessica walking down the hall. Sensing a scoop, Lois hurried toward them. "Diana! What are your chances of being elected queen?"

"Well, I am working very hard to win the support of the students. So, by Tyche's good fortune, I think my chances are as good as anyone's," Diana answered.

"Really? Your social media likes are zero—zilch—nada—no likes at all," Lois told her. "Care to comment?"

"What?" Zee gasped. She whipped out her cell phone and began scrolling furiously.

Satisfied that she'd stirred up news for tomorrow, Lois darted off in search of her next scoop.

"This can't be right! Traffic on your campaign page is at an all-time low!" Zee exclaimed.

Diana looked at her in confusion. "What campaign page? What traffic? There are no automobiles here," she said, staring up and down the hall.

Zee explained that she had created social media accounts for the campaign. Diana

was easily perplexed by the wonders of the internet, so Zee had taken responsibility for connecting her to an online audience.

Zee scrolled worriedly through the campaign feeds, showing Jessica the latest traffic data.

"Uh-huh. I see. Ah. Uh-oh. Oh no. Really? Ugh," Jessica said.

"What is wrong?" Diana asked. "Are there not enough of those emotional mojis?"

"The bottom line is that we need to win over the hearts of the student body," said Zee.

"Perhaps if I told them the story of the Tournament of Athena and Aphrodite and the Twenty-One Challenges," Diana suggested. "Among the Amazons, this rousing tale would be told while polishing armor and serve to bolster the bonds of sisterhoo—"

"WE KNOW!" Jessica and Zee said firmly.

The three girls walked in silence for a moment. Each was thinking of ways to help Diana win.

"I think you need something a bit more modern than an armor-polishing tale. Something like . . ." Jessica's voice trailed off as they turned a corner in the hall. Up ahead, Oliver Queen's campaign was in full swing. He stood in front of a flashy selfie booth, inviting students to join him.

"Take a selfie with a real leader!" Oliver called out. "As homecoming king, *I'll* make *you* look good." He placed a paper crown on his head and gestured to the fancy backdrop hanging behind him. The other students in the

hall were delighted. They pulled out their phones and lined up, eager to take a photo with Oliver.

"I hate to say it," Jessica whispered, "but that's a pretty genius campaign stunt."

"You're right," said Zee. "That's exactly the kind of thing we need to do for Diana."

"What about Oliver Queen? Now, there's a fella with moxie and a mind for marketing! What do you say? Is he the next homecoming king?" said Lois Lane, popping up in front of them.

"Where did she come from?" Jessica asked, startled, but before she could respond, Carol Ferris swooped in. She pushed Jessica aside and peered into Lois's phone camera. "There is only one candidate fit for king, and his name is Hal Jordan! HE WILL BE KING. HE WILL BE MINE!"

"Really?" said Lois. "Because I heard he broke up with you by text. Care to comment?"

Carol's eyes widened. She remembered the painful day when Hal had ended their relationship. He had tried to soften the blow by adding a smiley-face emoji to the text. That only made things worse. Carol was still

95

convinced that they belonged together, and she would use the tiara's wish to make him hers.

"I WILL BE QUEEN!" Carol shouted even louder. "AND HAL JORDAN WILL BE MY KING! NO ONE WILL COME BETWEEN US!"

"You heard it here first," Lois said as Carol turned on her heel and marched off, headed for the girls' bathroom.

Jessica shook her head. "I just don't know what she sees in Hal," she said to Diana and Zee. "I mean, who breaks up with someone by text?"

Before either girl could answer, they were interrupted by a whistling sound. It took Diana a moment to identify it. "Incoming!" she shouted, dragging Zee and Jessica with her to the floor.

Suddenly, several heart-shaped balls of energy exploded into the lockers behind them. Diana, Jessica, and Zee looked up to see

Star Sapphire hovering at the end of the hall. The Violet Lantern was angry, and she was glowering straight at them!

"How did she get here?" Zee asked.

"I do not know, Zee Zatara," Diana said. "But it appears that we have done something to offend her."

Diana's suspicions were confirmed when Star Sapphire fired off a second round of exploding hearts. The three girls rolled to their

feet and scrambled for cover behind a trophy case, while the rest of the students fled the hall. Even Oliver decided that it might be unwise to stick around. He folded up his selfie booth and scurried off.

"What is it we have done to bring on this attack of hearts?" Diana asked.

"Violet Lanterns get fierce when they think someone is standing in the way of love," said Jessica. "Maybe she heard Carol and flew to her rescue?" As a Green Lantern, Jessica knew Star's real identity, but she was honor bound not to reveal it.

"*Her* rescue? What about us?" Zee asked as another heart exploded nearby.

"It does seem that her purple rage is misdirected," Diana said. "But that leaves us no choice. We must protect the school."

Carefully, Zee peeked out from behind the trophy case to see Star Sapphire flying directly toward them. The rest of the hall was

completely empty. Zee quickly motioned to Diana and Jessica to follow her. They ducked into an empty classroom and transformed.

"You will not be queen, Diana!" Star shouted from the hallway. "You will not have my wish. You will not have my Hal!"

Green Lantern was the first to step back into the hall, holding a circular shield powered by her ring. She deflected Star Sapphire's energy blasts, while Wonder Woman and Zatanna sheltered behind her.

"How long can you hold it?" Zatanna asked.

"As long as you need," she answered, muscling her way forward. Soon, they were close to where Star Sapphire hovered. Wonder Woman leaped out from behind Green Lantern and charged toward the Violet Lantern with a fierce battle cry.

Star Sapphire was just about to launch another volley of blasts when suddenly she noticed that Diana was no longer there.

"What are you doing here, Wonder Woman? Where is Diana? This isn't your fight!" she said.

Wonder Woman skidded to a stop. She explained that Diana and her friends had run off in the commotion. Star Sapphire's temper faded. Now that her biggest competition for queen was no longer present, she gave up the fight.

"Tell her that I'll be back," Star said with a flip of her hair. She turned and flew down the hall, leaving a trail of purple light in her wake.

Green Lantern lowered her shield and said, "Never underestimate a super-villain with a crush."

Wonder Woman and Zatanna agreed. With the danger averted, the three super heroes hurried off to change. They didn't want to be late for third-period English.

Having been huddled behind a trash can at the end of the hall, Lois Lane emerged from hiding. She'd captured the whole confrontation on her live feed. It was sure to win the *Daily Planetoid* its biggest streaming audience ever! But when she looked at the feed, there were zero likes! That was when Lois noticed that she had no Wi-Fi signal!

"You gotta be kidding me!" she wailed.

The school's Wi-Fi had been knocked out by the fight with Star Sapphire. That meant that everything Lois had just filmed hadn't been posted! Lois wasn't sure which was worse: a super-villain in the fourth-floor hall or a day without an internet connection!

Chapter 9

Say Yes to the Dress and No to the Pantsuit . . . Unless You're an Amazon Princess

"**A**nd I thought fighting Catwoman was tough!" Zee Zatara exclaimed.

She and Jessica were standing outside a dressing room door at the Metropolis Mall. They were in a trendy clothing boutique, helping Diana choose a dress for the homecoming dance. But Diana wasn't making things easy. Inside the stall, she rejected every one of Zee's fashion choices.

"Great Gordian knot, I do not like how these

garments restrict my movement," Diana said through the door. "An Amazon must keep her sword arm free at all times."

"Diana, this is a dance, not a battle!" said Zee.

"I understand that, Zee Zatara. But can you not find me something functional?" Diana asked.

Zee folded her arms in frustration as Diana tossed yet another dress over the stall door. This one landed squarely on top of Zee's head. Jessica plucked the dress from Zee and added it to the return rack.

"Are you sure you don't like that one?" Jessica asked. "It's made out of sustainable fabric."

"It is like wearing the heavy chains of Prometheus," said Diana. "But this next one I like." She opened the door and emerged triumphantly from the stall.

Zee took one look at her and said,

"Absolutely not! You are NOT wearing a pantsuit to homecoming!"

"Why not?" asked Diana. "This jacket provides protection, and I am still able to kick and lunge in these pants."

"She does have a point," Jessica said.

"We do not kick and lunge at homecoming!" Zee replied. She would have argued further, but her phone rang. It was a video call from Babs, Kara, and Karen, who were still back at school.

"How is the repair going?" Diana asked, peering over Zee's shoulder into the screen. She could see her three friends on the roof of the school building. After Lois Lane's complaint, they were fixing the school's broadcast tower to restore the Wi-Fi.

"So far, so good. We're almost done," said Babs. She flipped the camera so that Diana, Jessica, and Zee could see the progress. In the distance, Kara hovered near the top of the tower. She was carrying Karen, who worked diligently with the tools hanging from her belt.

"How are the students doing without the internet?" Jessica asked.

"Don't you mean *what* are they doing without the internet?" Kara called out. "Answer: nothing."

"It sounds like they are taking a much-needed break from their infernal devices," said Diana.

"Those devices are what keep the peace," said Babs. "If we don't finish up soon, it's going to look like a post-apocalyptic future around here."

"I see," Diana said seriously. "Then perhaps

I will purchase protective pantsuits for all of us. We will match!"

Zee shook her head, exasperated. She decided to ignore Diana's comment and focus on the campaign instead. "I bet Oliver is freaking out right about now," she said. "What good is a selfie with him if no one has the Wi-Fi to post it?"

"That is why I am glad our focus is on school improvement," Diana said. "It is my hope that this repair will win me the hearts of my peers."

From the top of the broadcast tower, Karen

gave Babs a thumbs-up. Babs flipped a switch, and the hum of electricity crackled through the air. Diana, Jessica, and Zee heard the sound of students cheering in the background. Wi-Fi service was restored!

Babs didn't waste a moment. She whipped out a second phone, and her fingers danced across the screen. Moments later, the whole school received a text alert telling them that Diana Prince had saved the internet! It ended with the catchy campaign slogan "Diana Delivers!"

"Excellent work!" said Diana, thanking her friends.

Kara and Karen joined Babs at the bottom of the tower. Now that the internet was working again, they were ready to get back to campaigning.  Karen had *Diana Delivers!* buttons to make, while Kara planned to hang posters.

Babs would continue to post to social media using #voteprinceforqueen. With just twenty-four hours until the homecoming dance, every second counted.

Zee ended the call and turned back to Diana, who was admiring her pantsuit in the dressing room mirror. She and Jessica exchanged a look. It was going to be a long afternoon of fashion faux pas.

Later, on their way out of the mall, Diana, Zee, and Jessica had an unexpected encounter. They accidentally bumped into Selina, Doris, and Harleen, who were loaded down with shopping bags.

"Hey, watch where you're goin', toots!" Harleen said.

"Excuse me. I did not see you," said Diana. She pointed to their bags. "It looks like you are also shopping for the homecoming dance."

"You could say that," Selina purred.

"I have recently made a purchase at a store for professional women who value comfort," Diana told them. Zee covered her face with her hands.

"Yeah? We bought stuff, too," Doris said, holding up her bags. Selina stepped on her foot. She didn't want Doris to reveal anything about their shopping trip.

"You went dress shopping at Harvey's Hardware?" Jessica said, looking at Doris's bags.

"Harvey's Hardware? Why did we not go to this store, Zee Zatara?" Diana asked. "It sounds like they carry functional attire."

"Very functional," Selina said, swatting Doris's bags out of view. She didn't want the other girls to see what was inside. They would certainly question the selection of ropes, lockpicks, and grappling hooks.

"It just depends on the function," said Harleen with a giggle.

Diana nodded and wished them well. Selina and her friends were eager to be on their way. Fashion was the least of their worries. They had plans to make the homecoming dance a night the school would never forget.

Chapter 10

There's No Place Like Homecoming for an Epic Battle . . . and the Snacks Are Good, Too!

The night of the homecoming dance had finally arrived! A bright full moon hung low in the sky. Thanks to all the improvements, the school looked brand-new. Windows sparkled, lawns were freshly mown, and the gym was beautifully decorated in the style of an outer space adventure. The building looked almost as good as the students, who showed up dressed in their finest.

Diana, Zee, Babs, Kara, Jessica, and Karen

were also dressed to impress. Diana wore her pantsuit with pride, and even though Zee disagreed with her fashion choice, she had to admit that Diana looked good. The girls had more important things to think about than fashion, however. Tonight the Star of Andromeda would make its appearance! And where the tiara was, Catwoman and her crew were sure to follow.

But the thought of Catwoman was not enough to dampen the excitement. Soon,

the girls would learn who would be elected homecoming king and queen. They would finally see if all their hard work on Diana's campaign had paid off.

"This is Lois Lane, reporting live from the homecoming dance!" said the school's intrepid reporter. With the Wi-Fi repaired, she had quickly resumed her broadcast duties. She spotted Hal Jordan by the punch bowl and hurried over to him. "Hal, tonight's the night! What do you say, sport? Which one of these fellas has what it takes to be king?"

Hal flashed a brilliant smile at Lois and said simply, "Me."

"Check the polls," Lois said smartly. "You've got the looks but not the likes. You're running way behind Oliver Queen."

"What?" Hal said, whipping out his cell phone. He turned away from Lois to scroll furiously through his social media feed.

Lois moved on to interview Steve Trevor, a

visiting student from a nearby military school. Though Steve wasn't eligible to vote, he had his own ideas about who would be elected king. "All the candidates are just swell. There isn't a bad pick in the bunch! I'm sure the student body will make the best choice," he said brightly.

Lastly, Lois spoke to Barbi Minerva. The popular girl was annoyed that her ritzy theme for the dance hadn't won. So it was no surprise when she said, "I think the classiest, most glamorous candidate will win."

Lois was about to comment when suddenly the lights dimmed. The student body president took the stage. He picked up the microphone and cleared his throat. A hush fell over the students. This was the moment they'd all been waiting for.

"My fellow students, for the first time in the history of the school we have only one winning candidate," the president said. "Oliver Queen

is the first person ever to be elected both homecoming king *and* queen!"

"But the Wi-Fi! Diana delivered the Wi-Fi!" Zee said, shocked by the results. She was equal parts confused and disappointed. But Diana remained exuberant.

"You are right, Zee Zatara. I may not be queen, but I delivered many improvements to the school, and by Zeus, that is cause for celebration!" She hugged each of her friends and thanked them in turn. As for Oliver, Diana was the first to congratulate him.

The entire gym went completely wild with applause. Even Carol Ferris cheered happily . . . until she realized what Oliver's win meant for her. She had not been voted queen, and

there was no way she could make Hal Jordan her king. Carol's eyes narrowed and her hands began to shake with anger.

Oliver didn't notice. He grabbed the microphone and delivered his acceptance speech. "My loyal subjects, as your newly elected king *and* queen, how can I ever thank you?" he asked. "No, wait, I have an idea. I can treat you to the sight of *me* in my shining tiara, dancing with *me,* ruling together in peace and harmony with *me*!"

Zee rolled her eyes, but for Diana's sake, she smiled and applauded graciously. But just as Oliver took the stage to be crowned, the lights went out.

The students in the gym murmured in confusion. It was pitch black, and they heard a thumping noise, followed by a muffled squeal.

The lights flickered back on to reveal a very strange scene. Onstage, Oliver Queen was tied to a chair! Behind him, Catwoman and

Star Sapphire were caught in an intense tug-of-war over a . . . *punch bowl!!!!*

Meanwhile, Garth, so used to being overlooked, was now the center of attention. He stood right next to Oliver with the Star of Andromeda perched on his  head! With everyone looking at him, he realized that he was wearing the tiara. Immediately, he crossed his fingers and squeezed his eyes shut.

Catwoman and Star Sapphire howled in indignation! They tossed the punch bowl aside and snatched the tiara from Garth's head. Garth ran for cover as Giganta, Livewire, Poison Ivy, and Harley Quinn stormed the stage. They formed a chain behind Catwoman, adding their strength to hers to wrestle the tiara away from Star Sapphire. But Star wouldn't be stopped! Her love for Hal Jordan burned brightly and powered her ring. Even though she was outnumbered, her power ring made her strong.

"Pink pinto refried!" Babs exclaimed.

Diana and her friends ducked into the locker room and quickly transformed. Moments later, Wonder Woman, Supergirl, Batgirl, Zatanna, Green Lantern, and Bumblebee emerged! They charged toward the villains!

Catwoman spotted the super hero girls out of the corner of her eye. "As much as I love a catfight, Carol, this isn't the time!" she snarled.

"I told you not to call me that!" Star Sapphire snapped.

"Listen to me," Catwoman said. "You know

what happened the last time we played tug-
of-war. Those ridiculous goody-goodies took
the tiara. If we work together this time, we
can beat them!"

"Why should I trust you?" Star Sapphire
said, suspicious. "You don't deserve this
crown!"

"You're right. I don't deserve it," Catwoman
said. "That's why I plan to share it with all my
friends."

"You mean I'll get a wish from the tiara?" asked Star.

"Of course!" Catwoman purred. "Deal?"

Star Sapphire hesitated, but her love for Hal won out. "Deal!"

The villains turned to take on the super hero girls. . . .

Chapter 11

Let's Dance . . . and Try Not to Destroy the School

For Catwoman, Star Sapphire, and the other villains, their first act as partners in crime was to escape the gym with the Star of Andromeda. Catwoman placed the tiara on her head for safekeeping, while Star Sapphire created a diversion. She rose into the air and let loose a stream of heart-shaped blasts!

The super hero girls dodged the blasts and quickly moved to protect the students. With the power of her ring, Green Lantern conjured a giant umbrella to shield the crowd from the falling hearts.

"Uh-oh. Looks like love is in the air," Supergirl said, using her heat vision to pop the hearts one by one.

This gave the villains just enough time to push their way out of the gym. Star Sapphire was the last to leave, covering her exit with a brilliant burst of violet light that temporarily blinded everyone.

In the hallway, Catwoman and Star Sapphire went in one direction, while the rest of the villains split up in the hopes of dividing the super hero girls. But Wonder Woman was ready with a strategy of her own. "I will lead the students out of the gym to safety while you stop the villains," she told her team.

Zatanna raced after Catwoman and Star Sapphire. The tiara sparkled on Catwoman's head as she ran down the hall. That gave Zatanna an idea.

"Oorehctiws, oorehctiws!" she said, casting a spell of illusion. The air crackled as the magic began to work. When Catwoman looked up, she saw the tiara on Star Sapphire's head!

"Give me that!" she growled, taking a swipe at Star.

"What are you talking about?" said Star. To her, it looked like the tiara was on Catwoman's head—and it was glowing! "You're using up the wishes!" she shrieked.

"How can I wish when the crown is on your head?!" Catwoman snarled.

Zatanna smiled. Her illusion was working perfectly! The villains were fighting each other.

Meanwhile, Batgirl chased Harley Quinn into the school cafeteria. Harley cartwheeled over the lunch tables and hurled chairs at Batgirl.

"Have a seat, Batsy-Watsy!" she cackled.

Batgirl ducked and trailed the villain into the kitchen. The first thing Harley did was raid the

refrigerator. She wasn't hungry, though. She lobbed the leftover food at Batgirl, tossing bowl after bowl of cold, wet lunch in her direction.

"Time for a little indigestion!" said Harley Quinn.

"Why don't you chew on this?" Batgirl responded. She grabbed a stack of plates and sent them hurtling after Harley.

On the other side of the building, Supergirl's superhearing detected the crash of dishes in the lunchroom. But she already had her hands full—literally. She muscled Giganta across the weight room and slung the giant villain into the wall. All around them, barbells and dumbbells clattered to the floor. Giganta stumbled, dazed, but quickly climbed to her feet.

"So many dumbbells, huh?" Supergirl said with a smirk.

"I don't get it," Giganta told her.

"Exactly," said Supergirl, winding up to throw another punch.

Meanwhile, on the roof, Bumblebee squared off against Livewire.

"Beat it, bug! Before you get zapped!" Livewire said, flinging bolts of electricity from her fingertips. Bumblebee nimbly climbed the broadcast tower on the roof, dodging Livewire's blasts. When she reached the top, she used her high-tech suit to shrink to the size of an insect.

"Huh? Where'd she go?" Livewire asked. Bumblebee flew up behind her. She tapped a button in her suit. Suddenly, she was full size again! Livewire jumped, startled by her sudden appearance.

"Shocked you, didn't I?" Bumblebee said as she launched her stingers.

On the ground below, Green Lantern chased Poison Ivy into the greenhouse, where the villain felt right at home. She blew a handful of sleeping blossoms at Green Lantern, but the Lantern was ready for her. She used her power ring to create a blow dryer and blew the flowers back at Poison Ivy, beating her at her own game.

"You reap what you sow!" Green Lantern told her.

Meanwhile, Wonder Woman led the students out of the gym to safety. She gathered everyone underneath the lights of the football field and told them to remain calm. Then she doubled back to join the fight!

127

By that time, most of the super hero girls had driven off the villains. Without Catwoman to hold them together, Harley Quinn, Giganta, Livewire, and Poison Ivy decided it was more important to save themselves than to worry about the tiara. One by one they slipped off into the night, leaving Batgirl, Supergirl, Bumblebee, and Green Lantern victorious!

But Catwoman and Star Sapphire wouldn't give up! Zatanna had been keeping them busy with her disappearing tiara trick, but they were beginning to catch on. Catwoman touched a hand to her head and felt the tiara, which spoiled the illusion.

"Looks like your little magic show is over," she told Zatanna.

"You mean there's a wish left for me?" Star Sapphire said, her eyes widening with joy. With the illusion shattered, her hopes to make Hal Jordan her king had returned. Love swelled within her, and her powers grew stronger. She

conjured a giant heart, so big that it nearly filled the hallway, and sent it flying toward Zatanna.

With the huge heart bearing down on her, Zatanna flew swiftly back toward the gym. The tables had turned! Now it was Catwoman and Star Sapphire who gave chase.

They hadn't expected to meet Wonder Woman, however. At the last moment, she appeared and pulled Zatanna out of the heart's path. The huge blast of energy crashed through the wall of the gym, leaving a giant heart-shaped hole!

"Phew! That was close," said Zatanna. She thanked Wonder Woman.

"I did not want you to be heartbroken," Wonder Woman said with a twinkle in her eye.

"Was that a joke?" Zatanna asked, surprised.

But there was no time for small talk! Catwoman and Star Sapphire charged toward

129

them. Catwoman swiped at Wonder Woman with her claws. But Wonder Woman was ready for her. She blocked the blows with her gauntlets and delivered a few blows of her own! Wonder Woman kicked, spun, and chopped, backing Catwoman into the gym. Zatanna couldn't help but notice that Wonder Woman's fighting looked just like her dancing. Her moves weren't exactly graceful, but they were fierce!

One of those fierce moves knocked the tiara from Catwoman's head. The Star of Andromeda went flying across the gym. Zatanna moved to intercept it, but Star Sapphire got there first. She snatched the tiara from the air, placed it on her head, and squeezed her eyes shut to make a wish.

"Oh please, oh please, oh please, oh please," Star Sapphire whispered.

"This can't be good," Zatanna thought. She braced herself for the powerful magic that the

130

Star of Andromeda surely contained.

Seconds ticked by. . . . Absolutely nothing happened!

Star Sapphire howled in frustration!

"You used all the wishes!" she shouted, blaming Catwoman.

"*There are no wishes*, you violet dolt!" Catwoman said. "Did you seriously think that thing was magic?"

Star Sapphire's bottom lip quivered. Her purple aura began to fade. She took the tiara from her head and dropped it. With her hopes dashed,  Star Sapphire flew out of the gym.

Catwoman snatched the tiara and placed it back on her head. She wasn't interested in wishes, but she was interested in priceless jewels.

"Out of my way, Wonder Woman,"

Catwoman hissed as she leaped at her.

Suddenly, music blared from the speakers in the gym.

The music moved Wonder Woman. One, two, three . . . One, two, three . . . One, two, three. Her arms jerked and chopped through the air. Surprised by the strange moves, Catwoman was pummeled by a series of kicks and blows from odd angles.

As the villain went sprawling across the floor,

the tiara flew into the air. Wonder Woman drew her lasso and snagged it.

While all eyes were on the tiara, Catwoman slipped out and ran off into the night.

Chapter 12

Diana Delivers a Dance Sensation . . . and Will Always Be Homecoming Queen in Our Hearts

Batgirl clicked off the music with the remote-control app on her phone.

"Those were some moves!" Zatanna said as the heroes returned to the gym.

"I could not have succeeded without your dance training," Wonder Woman told her friends. "Those moves really came in handy on the field of battle!"

With the tiara recovered and the villains gone, the super hero girls changed back into their homecoming outfits. They walked out of the school toward the students gathered on the football field. Diana carried the tiara in her hands. Now that the villains had been defeated, it was time to celebrate.

"It's party o'clock, by my watch," said Babs.

"But the gym's in no shape for home-coming," Jessica pointed out.

"Why don't we have the dance out here?" Karen suggested. She looked across the field of students lit by the full moon.

"That is a great idea, Karen Beecher," Diana said. "Let us pick up where we left off."

Diana worked her way through the crowd until she found Oliver Queen. "I believe this crown is for you," she told him.

Oliver was thrilled when Diana placed the Star of Andromeda on his head. The first thing he did was close his eyes to make a wish. Everyone held their breath. . . .

"I won, and I look fabulous—it's everyone's wish come true!" Oliver proclaimed. "Now, let's dance!"

Babs whipped out her phone and tapped the screen. Music piped out through the speakers on the football field.

Oliver turned to Diana and said, "Even though I'm king and queen, it's tradition to share the first dance. Maybe you can show me

some of your dance moves." He extended a hand to Diana.

"I am happy to. Let us share this dance with all the students!" Diana said to the crowd.

"That's the smeltiest!" a student shouted.

"So smelty!" said another.

"Let's go Gorgon on it!"

"ANVIL DROP!"

Diana closed her eyes and let the music flow through her. She didn't move with an acrobat's grace, but she definitely danced with a warrior's heart.

Oliver copied Diana. He kicked, chopped, and spun, striking heroic poses between steps. "Is it just me, or do I look really good?" Oliver asked, jerking his arms.

Soon, the whole field of students was caught up in the latest dance craze. They called it the Diana.

"Looks like Diana got to kick off the first

dance anyway," Zee told her friends. She looked thoughtful for a moment. "I wonder who nominated her for homecoming queen."

Karen cleared her throat and spoke up. "I did," she said. "I couldn't think of anyone who'd make a better leader."

Babs, Kara, Jessica, and Zee all agreed. They couldn't have wished for a better queen.

On the other side of the football field, out of view, one student danced to the beat of his own drum. Garth, so often overlooked, danced with a beautiful fish girl. He couldn't believe it. Sometimes wishes did come true.